EMMA
Every Day

The Writing Contest

by C.L. Reid

illustrated by Elena Aiello

PICTURE WINDOW BOOKS

a capstone imprint

Published by Picture Window Books, a Capstone imprint
1710 Roe Crest Drive
North Mankato, Minnesota 56003
capstonepub.com

Library of Congress Cataloging-in-Publication Data
Names: Reid, C. L., author. | Aiello, Elena (Illustrator),
illustrator. |Reid, C. L. Emma every day. Title: The writing contest /
by C.L. Reid ; illustrated by Elena Aiello. Description: North Mankato,
Minnesota : Picture Window Books, 2023. | Series: Emma
every day | Audience: Ages 5-7. | Audience: Grades K-1. |
Summary: Her second place finish in a writing contest for
third graders disappoints Emma, a deaf girl, but her best friend
Izzie, who did not expect much, is thrilled to finish third,
so the girls decide to celebrate together. Includes an ASL
fingerspelling chart and a sign language guide.
Identifiers: LCCN 2021056928 (print) | LCCN 2021056929 (ebook)
| ISBN 9781666338645 (hardcover) | ISBN 9781666338669 (paperback)
| ISBN 9781666338652 (pdf) | ISBN 9781666338683 (kindle edition)
Subjects: LCSH: Deaf children—Juvenile fiction. | Creative
writing—Juvenile fiction. | Contests—Juvenile fiction. | Best
friends—Juvenile fiction. | CYAC: Deaf—Fiction. | Creative
writing—Fiction. | Contests—Fiction. | Best friends—Fiction. |
Friendship—Fiction. | LCGFT: Picture books. Classification: LCC
PZ7.1.R4544 Wr 2023 (print) | LCC PZ7.1.R4544 (ebook) | DDC [E]—dc23
LC record available at https://lccn.loc.gov/2021056928
LC ebook record available at https://lccn.loc.gov/2021056929

Image Credits: Capstone: Daniel Griffo, bottom left 28, top left 29,
bottom right, Margeaux Lucas, bottom right 28, top right 29, bottom
left 29, Randy Chewning, top left 28, top right 28

Design elements: Shutterstock: achii, Maric C, Mika Besfamilnaya

Special thanks to Evelyn Keolian for her consulting work.

Editor's note: Throughout the book, a few words are called out and
fingerspelled using ASL. Some of these words do have signs as well.

Designer: Nathan Gassman

TABLE OF CONTENTS

MEET EMMA

EMMA CARTER
Age: 8 Grade: 3

SIBLING
One brother, Jaden
(12 years old)

PARENTS
David and Lucy

BEST FRIEND
Izzie Jackson

PET
a goldfish named Ruby

favorite color: **teal**
favorite food: **tacos**
favorite school subject: **writing**
favorite sport: **swimming**
hobbies: **reading, writing, biking, swimming**

FINGERSPELLING GUIDE

MANUAL ALPHABET

Aa   Bb   Cc   Dd   Ee

Ff   Gg   Hh   Ii   Jj

MANUAL NUMBERS

0   1   2   3

Emma is Deaf. She uses American Sign Language (ASL) to communicate with her family. She also uses a Cochlear Implant (CI) to help her hear.

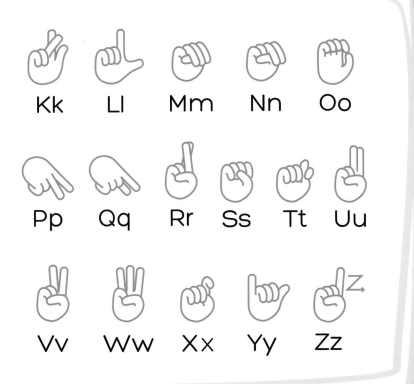

Kk Ll Mm Nn Oo

Pp Qq Rr Ss Tt Uu

Vv Ww Xx Yy Zz

4 5 6 7 8 9 10

Chapter 1

The Announcement

It was Tuesday, which meant

the class had media

time at school.

Emma and her best friend,

Izzie, loved library day. As they

entered the library, they stopped to

read the new announcements.

"Look! A writing contest!" Izzie signed, pointing.

Emma read the sign.

WRITING CONTEST

FICTION OR NONFICTION STORY

UP TO 250 WORDS, OPEN TO ALL THIRD GRADERS

1 PRIZE
FAMILY TICKETS TO THOMAS THEME PARK

2 PRIZE
FREE MEAL AT THE TACO HUT

3 PRIZE
FREE TREAT AT MARTA'S ICE CREAM

"I am definitely going to enter," Emma signed. "You should try too."

"I don't know," Izzie signed. "I am not a good writer."

"Yes you are! We have two weeks until the deadline. Let's both try," Emma signed.

"Okay," Izzie signed. "I will try. What will you write about?"

"I don't know," Emma signed. "Let's brainstorm."

The girls spent the rest of their media time making a list of ideas.

They looked at books. They did searches on the computers. They asked their friends.

By the end of media time, they both had a big list of ideas.

"Do you feel better about writing now?" Emma signed.

"I do," Izzie signed.

"I think I will win," Emma signed. "I can't wait to start."

Chapter 2

Ruby's World

When Emma got home, she went straight to her room. She wanted to start writing her story.

Emma looked at her list of ideas. She sat with her notebook and pencil ready. But none of the ideas excited her.

Emma looked at her fish, Ruby 🤟. She was swimming around the fishbowl.

"What can I write about, Ruby?" she asked.

Ruby stopped swimming, looked at Emma, then dived into a castle that sat at the bottom of the bowl. Ruby laughed.

Emma watched Ruby some more. Then an idea hit her!

"I will write about you, Ruby!" she said.

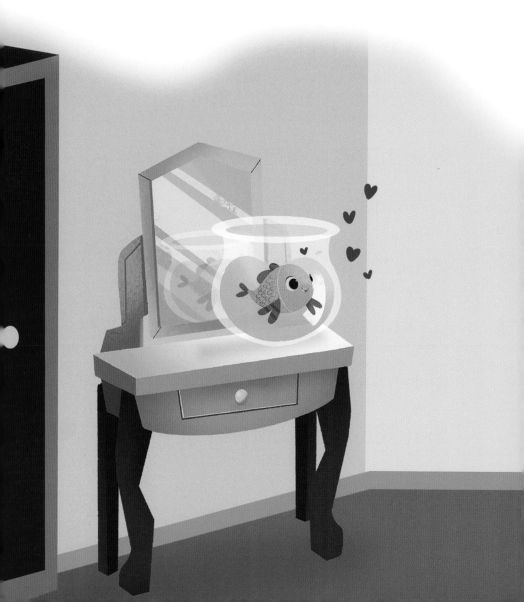

Emma began to write. She wrote about how Ruby was the wisest, funniest, and most loved goldfish in the world. She wrote about how Ruby was the best listener and never got bored or tired of listening.

Emma's pencil flew across the page. She wrote and wrote and wrote. At last, she set her pencil down and looked at her work.

"Done!"  Emma said. "Thank you for the idea, Ruby."

Emma ran downstairs and showed Dad her story.

"Will you check it for spelling mistakes, please?" Emma signed.

Emma waited while Dad read.

She knew it was a good story.

"I love it, but it needs a title," Dad signed.

"I forgot," Emma signed. She thought for a minute. "How about Ruby's World?"

"Perfect," Dad signed. "Now off to bed."

Emma pranced up the stairs. She took her Cochlear Implant (CI) off and climbed into bed. Emma dreamed about going to Thomas Theme Park.

Chapter 3

Treat Time

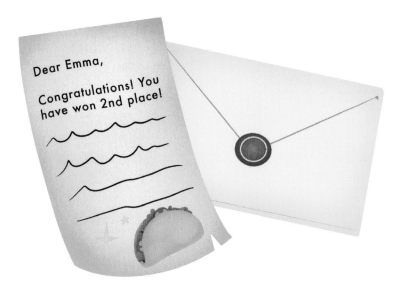

Dear Emma,

Congratulations! You have won 2nd place!

After a few weeks, the letter from the contest arrived. Emma tore it open and began to read. But after a minute, she blinked back tears of disappointment.

"I didn't win," she signed. She held up a little card. "I won a gift card  for a meal at The Taco Hut."

"Second place is still very good," Dad signed.

"But I thought I would win," Emma signed.

"You tried your best, so you did win," her dad signed.

"Yes, I tried my best," Emma signed. "And I am going to keep writing to get better."

"That's my girl!" her dad signed.

Just then the doorbell rang. It was Izzie!

"I won third place! I am so surprised!" she signed.

Emma was happy for her friend. It made her smile seeing how excited Izzie was.

"I am so happy for you! I got second place," Emma signed.

"Way to go! Now we can have tacos and ice cream to celebrate," Izzie signed.

"That is a great idea!" Emma signed.

"Congratulations to both of you," her dad signed. "Now get in the car. It is treat  time!"

LEARN TO SIGN

father

Touch thumb to forehead.

fish

Hold hand sideways
and wiggle.

happy

Make two small circles
at chest.

pencil

Place finger near mouth.
Slide fingers across palm.

celebration

Make X shapes and move
wrists in small circles.

library

Move L shape in a circle.

paper

Slide palms
together twice.

congratulations

Clasp hands together
and shake twice.

GLOSSARY

brainstorm—a way to come up with ideas or solutions in a group

Cochlear Implant (also called CI)—a device that helps someone who is Deaf to hear; it is worn on the head just above the ear

deadline—a time when something must be done

deaf—being unable to hear

fingerspell—to make letters with your hands to spell out words; often used for names of people and places

prance—to walk in a bouncing way

sign language—a language in which hand gestures, along with facial expressions and body movements, are used to communicate

TALK ABOUT IT

1. Izzie doesn't like writing. How do you think she felt when Emma said she should enter the contest?

2. What would you have said to Emma when she didn't win the contest?

3. Why do you think it's important for Emma to keep writing even after she didn't win the contest?

WRITE ABOUT IT

1. Izzie doesn't like writing because she doesn't think she's good at it. Write about something you want to get better at.

2. Do you relate better to Emma or Izzie in this story? Write five reasons you picked that character.

3. Write about a contest you would like to enter. Draw a poster about the contest to match your idea.

ABOUT THE AUTHOR

Deaf-blind since childhood,
C.L. Reid received a Cochlear
Implant (CI) as an adult to
help her hear, and she uses
American Sign Language (ASL) to
communicate. She and her husband have three
sons. Their middle son is also deaf-blind. Reid
earned a master's degree in writing for children
and young adults at Hamline University in St. Paul,
Minnesota. Reid lives in Minnesota with her
husband, two of their sons, and their cats.

ABOUT THE ILLUSTRATOR

Elena Aiello is an illustrator
and character designer. After
graduating as a marketing
specialist, she decided to study
art direction and CGI. Doing
so, she discovered a passion for
illustration and conceptual art. She works
as a freelancer for various magazines and
publishers. Aiello loves video games and sushi
and lives with her husband and her little pug,
Gordon, in Milan, Italy.

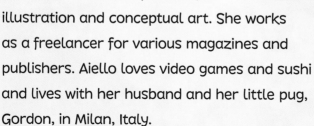